leapfrog

Bill's Baggy
Trousers

First published in 2000 by
Franklin Watts
338 Euston Road
London
NW1 3BH

Franklin Watts Australia
Level 17 / 207 Kent Street
Sydney
NSW 2000

A CIP catalogue record for this book is available
from the British Library.

ISBN 978 0 7496 3829 0

Series Editor: Louise John
Series Advisor: Dr Barrie Wade
Series Designer: Jason Anscomb

Printed in China

Franklin Watts is a division of
Hachette Children's Books
an Hachette Livre UK company.

Bill's Baggy Trousers

by Susan Gates

Illustrated by Anni Axworthy

FRANKLIN WATTS

LONDON•SYDNEY

Bill's mum bought him some new trousers.

The trousers were very big and baggy.

They had lots of pockets.

Bill's mum sent him to the shops.

"I can put the shopping
in my pockets," said Bill.

"I'd like some potatoes, please," said Bill to the shopkeeper.

The shopkeeper helped
Bill fill his pockets with
the potatoes.

"I can't walk!" said Bill.

"My trousers are much too heavy."

Bill took all the potatoes
out of his pockets.

Suddenly, the wind began
to blow up Bill's trousers.

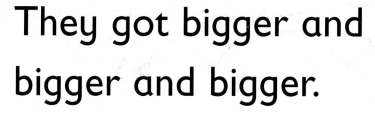

They got bigger and
bigger and bigger.

"Oh no!" shouted Bill.
"I'm floating away!"

Bill floated high up into the sky.

He floated over the
town ...

... and waved to his·mum in the garden.

Bill's mum didn't see him.

"Look at me, Mum!"
shouted Bill.

Suddenly, a bird pecked
Bill's trousers.

They went Sssssssssss ...

Bill's trousers got
smaller and smaller.

"Look out! I'm coming down," he shouted.

Bill landed next to his mum in the garden.

"You were quick!" she said.

Leapfrog has been specially designed to fit the requirements of the National Literacy Strategy. It offers real books for beginning readers by top authors and illustrators. There are 55 Leapfrog stories to choose from:

The Bossy Cockerel
ISBN 978 0 7496 3828 3

Bill's Baggy Trousers
ISBN 978 0 7496 3829 0

Little Joe's Big Race
ISBN 978 0 7496 3832 0

The Little Star
ISBN 978 0 7496 3833 7

The Cheeky Monkey
ISBN 978 0 7496 3830 6

Selfish Sophie
ISBN 978 0 7496 4385 0

Recycled!
ISBN 978 0 7496 4388 1

Felix on the Move
ISBN 978 0 7496 4387 4

Pippa and Poppa
ISBN 978 0 7496 4386 7

Jack's Party
ISBN 978 0 7496 4389 8

The Best Snowman
ISBN 978 0 7496 4390 4

Mary and the Fairy
ISBN 978 0 7496 4633 2

The Crying Princess
ISBN 978 0 7496 4632 5

Jasper and Jess
ISBN 978 0 7496 4081 1

The Lazy Scarecrow
ISBN 978 0 7496 4082 8

The Naughty Puppy
ISBN 978 0 7496 4383 6

FAIRY TALES
Cinderella
ISBN 978 0 7496 4228 0

The Three Little Pigs
ISBN 978 0 7496 4227 3

Jack and the Beanstalk
ISBN 978 0 7496 4229 7

The Three Billy Goats Gruff
ISBN 978 0 7496 4226 6

Goldilocks and the Three Bears
ISBN 978 0 7496 4225 9

Little Red Riding Hood
ISBN 978 0 7496 4224 2

Rapunzel
ISBN 978 0 7496 6159 5

Snow White
ISBN 978 0 7496 6161 8

The Emperor's New Clothes
ISBN 978 0 7496 6163 2

The Pied Piper of Hamelin
ISBN 978 0 7496 6164 9

Hansel and Gretel
ISBN 978 0 7496 6162 5

The Sleeping Beauty
ISBN 978 0 7496 6160 1

Rumpelstiltskin
ISBN 978 0 7496 6165 6

The Ugly Duckling
ISBN 978 0 7496 6166 3

Puss in Boots
ISBN 978 0 7496 6167 0

The Frog Prince
ISBN 978 0 7496 6168 7

The Princess and the Pea
ISBN 978 0 7496 6169 4

Dick Whittington
ISBN 978 0 7496 6170 0

The Elves and the Shoemaker
ISBN 978 0 7496 6581 4

The Little Match Girl
ISBN 978 0 7496 6582 1

The Little Mermaid
ISBN 978 0 7496 6583 8

The Little Red Hen
ISBN 978 0 7496 6585 2

The Nightingale
ISBN 978 0 7496 6586 9

Thumbelina
ISBN 978 0 7496 6587 6

RHYME TIME
Mr Spotty's Potty
ISBN 978 0 7496 3831 3

Eight Enormous Elephants
ISBN 978 0 7496 4634 9

Freddie's Fears
ISBN 978 0 7496 4382 9

Squeaky Clean
ISBN 978 0 7496 6805 1

Craig's Crocodile
ISBN 978 0 7496 6806 8

Felicity Floss: Tooth Fairy
ISBN 978 0 7496 6807 5

Captain Cool
ISBN 978 0 7496 6808 2

Monster Cake
ISBN 978 0 7496 6809 9

The Super Trolley Ride
ISBN 978 0 7496 6810 5

The Royal Jumble Sale
ISBN 978 0 7496 6811 2

But, Mum!
ISBN 978 0 7496 6812 9

Dan's Gran's Goat
ISBN 978 0 7496 6814 3

Lighthouse Mouse
ISBN 978 0 7496 6815 0

Big Bad Bart
ISBN 978 0 7496 6816 7

Ron's Race
ISBN 978 0 7496 6817 4